Volume 2

All-Time Favourite

FAIRY TALES

5-IN-1

Retold by

KEN SPILLMAN

Art by BETH PARROCHA

SCHOLASTIC
New York Toronto London Auckland
Sydney New Delhi Hong Kong

Dr Ken Spillman is the author of more than 60 books including the internationally popular Jake series. Based in Australia, Ken travels frequently and has spoken to more than 80,000 children in the past five years. He is a long-time advocate for writers and writing in the Asian region and actively supports organisations connecting marginalised children with the world of stories. For more information, visit: www.kenspillman.com.

Beth Parrocha is a children's book illustrator who loves colour. She has more than 50 children's books to her name. Come play with her as she brings your favourite book characters to life.

Published by Scholastic India Pvt. Ltd.
A subsidiary of Scholastic Inc., New York, 10012 (USA).
Publishers since 1920, with international operations in Canada, Australia, New Zealand, the United Kingdom, India, and Hong Kong.

For information regarding permission, write to:
Scholastic India Pvt. Ltd.
A-27, Ground Floor, Sigma Centre
Infocity-1, Sector 34, Gurgaon 122001 (India)

ISBN-13: 978-93-5103-769-9

First edition: November 2015

This reprint edition: April 2025

Printed in India at MicroPrints India, New Delhi

CONTENTS

Snow White and the Seven Dwarfs

Once upon a time, a Queen sat beside her castle's window. She was expecting a baby, and embroidering a little nightcap for it. Hoping for a daughter, she gazed out the window at the fallen snow. While doing so, she pricked her finger and drew blood.

'I do so wish for a little girl,' the Queen thought. 'May she have skin as white as snow, cheeks as red as blood, and hair as black and shiny as this window frame.'

The baby came and was indeed a little girl, looking just as the Queen had wished. Her skin glowed fair and her cheeks

were rosy. Her hair shone thick and black. The Queen called her daughter Snow White.

Alas, Snow White's mother died when the child was very young. When the King married again, his new Queen was beautiful and smugly proud of it. Often she would boast of being the most beautiful woman in the entire world, and no one would disagree.

One of the new Queen's wedding gifts was a magical mirror. She would stand before it and admire herself, sometimes for hours. Then she would say:

'Tell me, mirror, tell me true!
Who is fairest? Tell me who!'

Without fail, the mirror would reply:

'Of all the ladies in the land,
The fairest by far is you!'

The Queen took little notice of her stepdaughter, but the years passed and Snow White grew ever more beautiful.

Neither was her beauty skin deep. Her personality, wit and generosity charmed all who met her—except the vain Queen.

Standing in front of the mirror one day, Snow White's stepmother recited her usual question:

'Tell me, mirror, tell me true!
Who is fairest? Tell me who!'

This time, the mirror replied:

'You are fair and lovely, it is true.
But Snow White is even lovelier than you.'

The Queen flung herself on her bed, crazy with anger and envy. After many hours, she called her most trusted servant and ordered him to solve her problem forever.

'Take Snow White into the woods,' she snarled. 'Take a hunting knife to her, and never tell a soul.'

The servant led the girl away. Into the woods they went. Snow White had not suspected that her stepmother was plotting murder, and when she realised what the servant was about to do, she screamed and begged for her life.

The man's heart melted. 'I will not hurt you, child. I cannot.' Finding a rabbit in a trap, he smeared its blood on his knife to show the Queen. Then he left Snow White to fend for herself in the wild forest.

Terrified, she wandered into the mountains, weeping quietly and jumping at every noise. When a twig snapped under her feet, she believed a bear would seize her. The wind roared and she imagined wolves.

Eventually Snow White came to a cottage. Finding it empty, she crept inside. Everything was neat and tidy. A cloth was spread on the table and on it there were seven little plates. There were seven bread rolls and seven little tumblers. By the wall stood seven little beds.

As Snow White was hungry, she tore a piece from each roll and took a mouthful from each tumbler. She tried all the little beds, and the seventh suited her perfectly. She tucked herself in and went to sleep.

After dark, the cottage's owners returned. There were seven of them, each one a dwarf who spent his days digging for gold in the mountains. They lit their seven lamps, and saw that all was not right.

The first dwarf asked, 'Who has been sitting on my stool?'

The second dwarf asked, 'Who left crumbs on my plate?'

'Someone has picked at my bread,' the third dwarf said.

'And mine!' said the fourth.

'Someone has been fiddling with my fork,' complained the fifth.

The sixth dwarf remarked that his spoon was sitting crooked, while the seventh saw that the drink in his tumbler was low.

By then, the first dwarf had carried his lamp over to his bed. 'Who has been lying on my bed?' he wondered aloud. Before long, his companions were looking at their own beds and repeating his words.

The seventh dwarf saw the peaceful face of Snow White in a deep sleep. The rest came quickly, holding their lamps over Snow White and whispering: 'Good heavens! How pretty she is!'

They did not wake her. The seventh dwarf slept on a rug by the fire and, in the morning, Snow White told them her story. The dwarfs were surprised that she was royalty, and shocked at her treatment by the Queen.

'Such a cruel stepmother,' one said.

'Such jealousy,' said another.

Wanting Snow White to be safe, they urged her to stay in their little house and promised to care for her. Each day, they went digging for gold. Each day, they warned: 'The Queen may yet learn where you are. Bolt the door and don't open it for anyone.'

Thinking Snow White was dead, the Queen was confident her beauty was unequalled. Her anger with the magic mirror disappeared, so she once again invited its compliments:

'Tell me, mirror, tell me true!
Who is fairest? Tell me who!'

Unable to lie, the mirror replied:

'You are fair and lovely, it is true.
But Snow White, in hiding, is lovelier than you.'

The Queen realised the servant must have betrayed her. She pestered the mirror for details of all it could see, and immediately began scheming to do what her servant did not.

The following day, she disguised herself and travelled to the mountains to find the home of the dwarfs. Knocking at the door, she called: 'Laces, hairpins, bobbins for sale! Combs and brushes of the best quality!'

Snow White remembered the dwarfs' warning, but was sure the old woman meant no harm. She unbolted the door.

'Your hair is so thick and long!' said the woman. 'These brushes will make your day easier.'

Snow White smiled. 'May I try one?' she asked, not suspecting that the wicked woman had dipped them all in

poison. As soon as the brush touched her head, Snow White fell and lay unmoving on the ground.

'That's the end of her,' the Queen said, and made her way back to the palace.

The dwarfs found Snow White slumped by the door, but rejoiced to find that she was still alive. Her thick hair had wiped poison from the comb before it touched her scalp, and she recovered to tell the dwarfs what had happened. Carefully they washed Snow White's hands and hair, and she became well again.

The Queen, meanwhile, was astonished to be told by her mirror:

'You are fair and lovely, it is true.
But Snow White lives, and is lovelier than you.'

Trembling with rage, she began scheming again. This time, she poisoned an apple, dressed herself as an orchard keeper and returned to the cottage in the mountains.

When Snow White heard a knock at the door, she put her head out of the window and saw the woman with her basket of apples. 'Madam,' she called, 'I cannot open the door, for the dwarfs have told me not to.'

'As you wish,' said the terrible woman, coming to the window. 'But I will leave you this fine apple. Tell me how you liked it when I come this way again.'

'No,' said Snow White, 'I dare not take it.'

'Silly girl!' answered the woman. 'What are you afraid of? Do you think it is poisoned? Look—I shall take a bite myself.'

The Queen had been careful to poison only half of the apple. She bit into the good side and held out the apple for Snow White. It looked delicious, and the woman was munching with gusto. Snow White could resist no longer, and bit into the other side.

'This time, nothing will save you,' said the Queen. Snow White fell to the floor and the Queen went home to her mirror, which at last told her:

'Of all the ladies in the land,
By far you are fairest—only you!'

The seven dwarfs found Snow White by the window, no longer breathing. They loved her dearly, and felt sorrow beyond belief. Together they lifted her up, straightened her hair and washed her lovely face.

The dwarfs knew they must bury her, but were not ready for the final parting. Days passed and Snow White's cheeks were still rosy, her face looking just as it had while she lived.

'Snow White was always special,' said one of the dwarfs. 'In death she is a miracle. We will never bury her in the cold ground.'

The dwarfs made Snow White a coffin of glass. They wrote her name on it in gold, and also noted that she was a King's daughter. Finally the coffin was placed on a hill outside and the dwarfs took turns watching over it. Every day, birds and animals gathered around. Snow White's beauty did not fade. Even now she was as white as snow, with bright cheeks and hair the colour of ebony. Flowers sprouted on the hill where she lay.

One day, a Prince from another kingdom came past with his men. The Prince gazed on Snow White's delicate face and was suddenly lost in love. He read what was written in golden letters and asked the dwarfs if he could take her away.

At first, they refused—but they saw the Prince's love and agreed when he promised to build Snow White a dazzling memorial at his father's palace.

The Prince's men lifted the coffin and bound it to a horse. The Prince said farewell to the dwarfs and the men started

off. The coffin jolted and, to the surprise of all, Snow White coughed up a piece of apple. She pushed a hand against the coffin's lid and sat up.

'What is happening?' Snow White asked.

The Prince and the dwarfs were overcome with happiness. 'You're alive!' the Prince cried. 'And you will be safe with me. Come to my father's palace and be my wife. I will love you forever.'

Snow White turned to the dwarfs. 'In another kingdom,' she said, 'there will not be a need to worry about my stepmother. You have taken good care of me. What do you say?'

The dwarfs wanted only the best for Snow White. Snow White agreed to the Prince's proposal and rode off with him.

At the palace, a grand wedding was planned, with no expense spared. The Prince's father invited other Kings and Queens from neighbouring lands—including the Queen who was Snow White's jealous stepmother.

As the Queen dressed in her finest clothes for the wedding, she again spoke to the mirror:

> 'Tell me, mirror, tell me true!
> Who is fairest? Tell me who?'

Said the mirror:

'Your beauty, my Queen, you cannot hide.

But lovelier still is the Prince's young bride.'

Hearing this, the Queen hurled a book at the magic mirror, smashing it into a thousand pieces. Her curiosity was so great that she still set out for the next kingdom to see the bride for herself.

The wedding scene was magnificent, the seven dwarfs having pride of place at the front. Snow White's stepmother watched and waited for the bride to lift her veil. When she saw that the Prince's bride was none other than Snow White, the surprise was too much. She fainted, hit her head on the stone floor and did not move again.

Snow White and her Prince lived and reigned happily over that land for many years, and had seven lovely children. The seven dwarfs, meanwhile, were honoured and rewarded. A little palace was built in place of their mountain cottage, furnished with luxuries. Snow White's children loved to play in it, and learned much about kindness from these small men, who truly possessed the biggest of hearts.

Little Red Riding Hood

There was once a pretty village girl, and she was greatly loved by all. Her grandmother lived alone in another village beyond a wood, and believed her to be the greatest gift an old woman could have. She made the child a cloak of red velvet with a fur-lined hood. The girl wore it wherever she went, and was soon known around the district as Little Red Riding Hood.

One day, Little Red Riding Hood's mother baked some cupcakes and asked her to take them to her grandmother.

'A nice woodcutter told me that she is ill,' the mother said. 'Please ask whether there is anything she needs.'

Little Red Riding Hood started off towards her grandmother's house, humming a sweet melody and with the basket of cakes swinging on her arm. She had not been walking long when her song caught the ear of that wily fellow, Mr Wolf. It was three days since he had last eaten, and he licked his lips.

'I'd like to gobble her up on the spot,' he thought. 'But there are woodcutters nearby and she might scream. Better to befriend her, and be patient.'

Mr Wolf stood in her path and smiled his toothy smile. Little Red Riding Hood smiled back sweetly at him. She knew how dangerous his kind could be, but saw that he wanted to be friendly.

'Child, where are you off to on this bright sunny day?' Mr Wolf asked.

'To visit my poor grandmother,' Little Red Riding Hood replied. 'We have heard that she may be ill.'

'Where does she live?' Mr Wolf enquired.

Little Red Riding Hood named the little village where her

grandmother lived. 'It is the first cottage you come to, just beyond the wood,' she added.

'But I know that house well!' Mr Wolf exclaimed. 'And I know a short cut. Follow me and I will show you.'

'Oh, I'm sorry Mr Wolf,' said Little Red Riding Hood. 'My mother forbids me from taking any other path. But thank you for offering help.'

Mr Wolf again smiled his toothy smile. 'What a good girl you are,' he said. 'But I have an idea. You take this path and I shall take my short cut, and we will see who arrives first. That way, your mother might send you by another path next time.'

This seemed very sensible to Little Red Riding Hood, so she agreed.

Off went Mr Wolf, while Little Red Riding Hood continued on her way. The wolf kept up a brisk pace, while the little girl amused herself by running after butterflies, plucking flowers and gathering berries.

When Mr Wolf arrived at the grandmother's cottage, he knocked on the door. There was no answer, so he knocked a little harder.

'Who is it?' croaked the old woman.

'It is your granddaughter, Little Red Riding Hood,' answered Mr Wolf in a high voice, imitating the child. 'My mother has baked you some cakes.'

'The door is unlocked, my darling girl,' the old woman said. 'Come inside.'

Mr Wolf found the grandmother in her bed and, in his fierce hunger, gobbled her up at once. Then he put on her clothes, dressed himself in her nightcap, drew the curtains and tucked himself into her bed.

Little Red Riding Hood tapped at the front door moments later.

'Who's there?'

Mr Wolf's gravelly voice frightened Little Red Riding Hood at first, but she remembered that her grandmother may have a terrible cold. She answered as she always did. 'It is your granddaughter, Little Red Riding Hood. I have brought some cakes from my mother, and some flowers and berries from the wood.'

'Come, child,' returned the strange voice. 'Put your goodies on the table and come to my bedroom.'

Little Red Riding Hood found her grandmother hunched

up in bed, with her nightcap pulled down over her face. 'Some woodcutters told us you have been sick,' she said. 'Mother wants to know whether there is anything we can bring you.' Drawing back the curtains, she sat at the bedside and was taken aback to see how different her grandmother looked when she wasn't up and dressed.

'Grandmother, what long ears you have!'

'All the better to hear you with, child.'

'Grandmother, what large eyes you have!'

'All the better to see your lovely face, my little girl.'

'Grandmother,' she exclaimed, 'what long arms you have!'

'All the better to embrace you with!'

'Grandmother, what large teeth you have!'

'All the better to eat you with!'

With these words, the wicked Mr Wolf sprang up and set upon Little Red Riding Hood, swallowing her right up. Now extremely full, he lay down again on the grandmother's bed and began to snore loudly.

Soon afterward a woodcutter came by—the very same man who had spoken to Little Red Riding Hood's mother of the old woman's illness. He smiled to himself at the sound of

her snoring so loudly, and decided to see whether she had enough wood for her fire.

Finding the door unlatched, he went into the cottage. He knocked gently on the bedroom door and then poked his head around it. Seeing the bloated wolf, he crept up and slit its throat.

'Oh, Mr Wolf,' he moaned, 'you have eaten that poor, defenceless old woman.'

Intending to skin the wolf and sell its fur at the market, the woodcutter took a pair of scissors and began to cut open the wolf's stomach. When he had made just two small snips, he saw a swatch of red velvet. With a few snips more, Little Red Riding Hood unfolded herself and stepped out of the wolf.

'Oh, thank you kind sir! How dark it was inside Mr Wolf—and I am frightened of the dark.'

Startled, the woodcutter then worked with Little Red Riding Hood to help the grandmother out of the wolf. Quite remarkably, she was no worse for the experience and insisted that all three sit down to celebrate with tea and some of the cupcakes Little Red Riding Hood had brought.

Later, the woodcutter accompanied the girl back to her village.

That night, Little Red Riding Hood thought to herself: 'As long as I live, I will never trust the smile of a wolf.'

Hansel and Gretel

Hansel and Gretel lived in a cottage with their father and a cruel stepmother. Their father was a poor woodcutter, and the children often heard their stepmother complaining that he made too little money to feed them. Most nights, the stepmother sent Hansel and Gretel to bed with only a piece of bread to share.

Lying awake hungry one night, Hansel and Gretel heard their father and stepmother talking.

'I will grow weak working on an empty stomach,' grumbled their father.

'I'm the one who collects the wood you cut,' replied his wife. 'Do you expect me to starve myself to feed your children? It is hardly my fault that you cannot earn a decent living.'

'I'm a humble woodcutter like my father. I know nothing else. What will become of us?'

'One day, all of us will die of starvation,' the stepmother grumbled. 'You should cut some wood and make coffins for us. If we are to live, the children must go.'

Hansel and Gretel were frozen in horror by their stepmother's words. They wished she had never met their widowed father and come suddenly into their lives. When the stepmother spoke again, she spoke pure evil.

'Tomorrow we must take them deep into the forest,' she told their father. 'If we build a fire, give them some bread and tell them to wait—they'll never find their way home again. We shall be free of them.'

'No!' their father protested. 'How shameful it would be to leave my children all alone. Bears or wolves would tear them to pieces!'

But the woman kept at him, wearing down his resistance. When finally he agreed to her plan, Gretel began to weep.

Hansel knew he must do something.

'Don't cry—I will never let such terrible things happen,' he said.

As soon as their father and his wife fell asleep, Hansel put on his coat and slipped out the door. The moon glowed brightly and the white pebbles that lay around their cottage shone like silver coins. Hansel filled his coat pockets with them and returned to his bed.

'We must be brave,' he told Gretel. 'I have a plan.'

Next morning, the stepmother woke the two children. 'Get up,' she said harshly, 'we are going with your father.'

Hansel's coat was heavy with pebbles as they trailed the adults through thick forest. Whenever Hansel was certain they wouldn't see, he dropped a pebble to mark their path. At last they came to a clearing, where their father built a fire and stacked wood for the children to throw on it. Their stepmother gave them half a loaf of bread, and with it some parting words. 'Do not eat it all at once—the day will be long.'

Gretel saw a tear in her father's eye as he picked up his axe and turned to leave, his wife by his side. Again Gretel wept, knowing that he intended to go along with their stepmother's plan, but again Hansel told her to be brave.

'Perhaps they'll change their minds. And if they don't, I know I can find the way home.'

Hansel and Gretel huddled by the fire. They shared the bread when the sun was high, too hungry to save even a crust for the evening. Hansel stoked the fire with the wood their father had left, and then they closed their eyes and slept.

It was quite dark when they woke, and the fire had burned low.

'They have deserted us,' Gretel wailed. 'How can we ever survive?'

Hansel's heart was heavy but he steadied his voice and said: 'When the moon rises I'll show you why I was dragging my feet this morning. We will find our way home, I promise.'

When the moon was overhead, Hansel took his sister's hand and led her first to one pebble, then another. The pebbles captured the moonlight and lit the long walk home. They knocked at the cottage door, and the stepmother let them in.

'Wicked children,' she scolded, 'you should have waited for us to return. You could have been lost forever!'

Hansel and Gretel knew the woman felt only bitter disappointment that they had returned safe and sound. They saw relief on their father's face as he hugged them to his

chest, but not long afterward they heard their stepmother scheming again.

'We will take them even deeper into the woods,' she spat. 'Never will I starve myself to feed such ragamuffins, no matter what you think.'

Hansel and Gretel crept to the door that night, intending to gather pebbles. They found the door locked and the key nowhere to be found. Hansel promised his sister he would think of something else. Later, he went to the kitchen and filled his coat pockets with bread.

Before dawn, the stepmother pulled Hansel and Gretel out of bed. She was very, very angry.

'Wicked children, how dare you steal bread? Today, you will not be given a single bite more.'

Gretel protested their innocence, but understood when she saw Hansel dropping crumbs from his pocket as they trudged into the forest. Deeper and deeper they went until Hansel had only a few crumbs left.

'Sit here and rest,' the stepmother said, while her husband lit a fire. 'When we are ready, we will fetch you. Do not be so foolish as to leave this spot, for you will surely get lost.'

When the adults had gone, Gretel spoke up. 'I know your plan, Hansel—but bread crumbs are not like white pebbles. They'll be eaten by birds and mice before nightfall.'

Hansel saw that his sister was right. 'Then we will go home right now,' he said.

They started back but it was too late. The forest was thick with birds and they had already feasted happily.

'It doesn't matter,' Hansel kept saying to Gretel, 'we will find our way while it is daylight.'

But the children walked all day and then through the night, and still couldn't find their way out of the forest. By morning they were so tired that they could not drag themselves any further, so they curled up under a tree and went to sleep.

Later they woke to the sound of a snow-white bird, singing sweetly on a branch above. It was the most beautiful bird Hansel and Gretel had ever seen. When it flew off, they ran after it. It led them to a small and pretty cottage, nestled in a glen. As Hansel and Gretel came closer, they were astonished to see that the cottage was made of bread and cakes, with window panes of candied sugar.

'We will have a delicious feast,' Hansel rejoiced. 'We will

start with bits of wall, and finish by sharing a window!'

They had scarcely begun when the cottage door opened and an old woman came out. Hansel and Gretel were frightened and dropped what they held in their hands, but the woman spoke kindly to them.

'Children, don't be afraid! Come in and eat in the warmth of my home.'

She led them inside and showed them to a table spread with pancakes, honey, apples and nuts. Then she poured two glasses of milk.

The woman seemed warm-hearted and Hansel and Gretel did not suspect for a moment that she was really a wicked witch, even more evil than their stepmother. She had a great appetite for children, and had built her house of bread and cakes to tempt girls and boys who were lost. The witch made them plump with sugary treats before roasting them in her huge oven for dinner.

In the back room were two snug little beds. After eating their fill, Hansel and Gretel tucked themselves in, wondering whether they had found heaven. As they slept, the witch crept in. She looked at their soft pink cheeks and licked her lips. 'So

HoNey
NuTS

tender and tasty,' she thought.

Suddenly the witch gathered up Hansel with her rough hands and thrust him into a little cage she kept hidden under the bed. He shouted and woke Gretel.

'Fetch water,' the witch ordered Gretel. 'I shall boil it and cook something nice for your brother.'

Gretel screamed at the sight of her brother in a cage, but the witch made her do as she was told. Each day, the witch cooked a big meal for Hansel, while Gretel was given his leftovers. And each day, the witch would ask Hansel to poke an arm through the mesh of his cage so that she could squeeze it.

'You need more fattening,' the witch would say, and the children would not know why.

Eventually, the witch could wait no longer. 'Whether he is fat or thin, I will eat your brother today,' she told Gretel. 'It is far too long since I tasted the juicy flesh of a child.'

Tears ran down Gretel's cheeks. She felt sure that she and her brother had been born only to suffer until the end. 'Dear God,' she cried, 'if we'd been eaten by wild beasts in the forest, at least we would have died together.'

'Fuss and noise won't help you,' the witch said. 'Bring more

wood for my oven. I will bake some bread to eat with the boy when he is cooked.'

Very slowly, Gretel fetched and stacked the wood, desperate to think of a way to save her brother. The witch soon lost patience with her. 'Stoke the fire and test the oven,' she ordered. 'See if it is hot enough to bake the bread.'

Gretel could think only of escape. She wanted to run into the forest but knew she could never leave poor Hansel to be cooked in the cage. The witch's keys were in an apron pocket, and Gretel had no idea how she might get them.

'Well? Is the oven hot? Tell me now, you foolish child,' shrieked the witch. 'Or I shall eat you with your brother.'

Gretel could barely speak, so the witch opened the oven herself. As she leaned forward to test the temperature, Gretel felt a surge of energy and fury. She leapt forward, pushing the screaming witch completely inside. Gretel heaved the oven's iron door into place and bolted it quickly. Then she ran to the cage.

'Hansel, the witch is dead! We're saved!' She told her brother what the witch had planned—and Hansel admitted he had known it from the moment he was caged.

When the oven fire burned down, nothing remained of the witch but ashes. Gretel raked through them to find the blackened keys. She tried one after another in the lock of the cage until she heard it click open. Hansel sprang out, dancing around his sister with joy and relief.

'Let's see what locks these other keys open,' said Hansel.

To the children's surprise, there were secret cupboards all around the cottage, each containing precious stones and pearls. 'These are better than pebbles,' laughed Hansel, filling his pockets and shovelling them into Gretel's pockets too. 'When we give these to Father, our stepmother will never again have reason to complain about being poor. There will be plenty of food for us all.'

Finding their way home was no easy task, but the children ate well from a bag packed with the witch's cakes. Alert for wild animals, they walked for days and finally came upon a familiar trail of white pebbles which led to their cottage.

They began to run and burst through the door, falling into their father's arms. He had lived in misery since leaving the children in the forest, and had driven his hateful wife out of his life forever. Gretel shook her coat, and pearls and precious stones rolled upon the floor. Hansel emptied his pockets too, knowing their sorrows were ended.

From that day forward, Hansel and Gretel wanted for nothing and lived together in great happiness.

Goldilocks and the Three Bears

The Three Bears were proud of their fine cottage in the woods. Papa and Mama Bear worked hard to keep everything just so—and Little Bear was the neatest and tidiest little bear they could have wished for.

Almost everything in the house could be seen in three sizes. Each bear had a special porridge bowl—a huge bowl for Papa Bear, a medium bowl for Mama Bear, and quite a small one for Little Bear. There were three sizes of spoons and three comfortable chairs to relax in—a big one for Papa Bear, a middle-sized one for Mama Bear, and a low one for Little Bear.

Upstairs, each of the Three Bears had a special bed too. Little Bear's bed was only just big enough to keep him snug and warm. Mama Bear's bed was twice as big, and Papa Bear's bed seemed, to Little Bear, really rather enormous.

One beautiful spring morning, when their porridge had been set on the table, the Three Bears went for a walk in the sunshine. At that very same time, an adventurous young girl had wandered deep into the woods searching for flowers. Known as Goldilocks for her long yellow hair, the girl was surprised to come upon such a pretty cottage so far from her village, and curious to see who might live there.

Goldilocks peeped through a window, and then through the keyhole. Seeing nobody, she tested the latch. The door was unlocked, for the Three Bears were good bears who welcomed friends and had no reason to expect unwanted visitors.

'Hello?' Goldilocks called. 'Is anybody home?'

There was no reply. Goldilocks looked around and saw how charming the cottage was, with three sizes of everything, all arranged so perfectly in place.

'Hello?' she called again, eager to meet new friends.

Again there was no reply. Tempted to explore a little more,

Goldilocks left her posy of flowers near the door and went inside. She knew that she shouldn't touch anything, but the porridge looked wonderfully inviting and Goldilocks suddenly felt hungry.

Surely, Goldilocks thought, *whoever lives in this fine house would not mind sharing a little breakfast?*

First she tasted the porridge in the big bowl of Papa Bear. It was too hot for her and burned her tongue.

Next, Goldilocks tasted the porridge in the middle-sized bowl. This was really quite cold, because Mama Bear had served herself from yesterday's leftovers.

Goldilocks then tasted the porridge of Little Bear. It was neither too hot nor too cold, but just right. She intended to have just a spoonful but in no time she had eaten it all up.

Feeling quite full, Goldilocks decided to sit for a while. First she climbed into the great big chair of Papa Bear.

'This chair is too big,' she murmured, getting up to try Mama Bear's medium chair instead.

Mama Bear's chair was also too big, and it creaked whenever she moved.

'This chair is too creaky,' she decided. She stood back up

and went over to Little Bear's dainty chair.

Little Bear's chair was neither too big nor too creaky, but just right. Contented, Goldilocks sat in it until it collapsed without warning. She untangled herself from broken pieces of chair and, still wanting to rest, went upstairs to the Three Bears' bedroom.

First she lay in the bed of Papa Bear. It looked very grand and snug, but she soon found the mattress uncomfortable.

'This bed is too hard,' she said, climbing out again.

The medium bed was next, but Mama Bear liked her mattress and pillows to be very soft. Goldilocks sank deep into the bed and got straight up.

'This bed is too soft,' she sighed. She was not only full of porridge, but also tired, and just a little annoyed.

Goldilocks tried the bed that belonged to Little Bear. She was glad to find that it was neither too hard nor too soft, but just right. She covered herself and lay there till she fell fast asleep.

When the Three Bears returned to their cottage for breakfast, they were surprised to find the front door open and a posy of flowers by the door.

'That's strange,' said Papa Bear. His voice was gruff, though in fact he was gentle and kind.

Inside, the Three Bears looked around. Goldilocks had left Papa Bear's big spoon standing in his porridge.

'Somebody has been eating my porridge!' Papa Bear boomed.

Mama Bear then looked at her middle-sized bowl. Her special spoon had also been dipped into the porridge, and was now lying crooked on the table. 'Somebody has been eating my porridge, too!' she exclaimed.

Little Bear looked at his own bowl and saw that all the porridge was gone. 'Somebody has been eating my porridge,' he said in his much smaller voice, 'and that naughty somebody has eaten it all up!'

While Little Bear was still looking at his empty bowl, Papa Bear and Mama Bear searched around to see if anything else in the house had been disturbed, or even perhaps stolen.

Papa Bear saw that the cushion on his chair was no longer straight. 'Someone has been sitting in my chair!' he grumbled loudly.

Mama Bear's cushion had also been moved. 'Somebody has

been sitting in my chair!' she said, sounding a little anxious.

Little Bear had now joined them, and was shocked to see that his own chair had been broken into pieces. 'Somebody has been sitting in my chair,' he complained, 'and naughty somebody has broken it!'

The Three Bears were now quite worried. Instead of just one uninvited guest, Papa Bear and Mama Bear thought there might be two or three, and that they may still be hiding in the cottage. They spoke in hushed tones, which was quite difficult for Papa Bear, and crept up the stairs to the bedroom.

Goldilocks had left the covers of Papa Bear's bed pulled back. 'Somebody has been lying in my bed!' Papa Bear protested. He had forgotten his attempt to be quiet, but Goldilocks did not stir.

Mama Bear looked at her bed and saw the shape Goldilocks had left in her soft mattress. 'Somebody has been lying in my bed too!' she observed with alarm.

When Little Bear came to look at his bed, which was last in line, he saw the covers pulled up over the same shape of a girl. On his pillow, he saw the long yellow hair of Goldilocks.

'Somebody has been lying in my bed—and naughty

somebody is still there!' Little Bear cried.

Woken by the shrill voice of Little Bear, Goldilocks opened her eyes and sat up. The sight of the Three Bears alarmed her, for she hadn't imagined that such a dear little cottage, with everything so neat and orderly, might belong to creatures so different from herself.

Though the bears made no move, Goldilocks sprang up and jumped out the window. She took quite a tumble on landing but ran home, not once stopping to catch her breath.

Goldilocks would never again wander alone in the forest, and the Three Bears never saw her again.

Beauty and the Beast

There was once a rich trader with three sons and three daughters. He was a good father, and spared no expense in the care and education of his children.

The youngest daughter was strikingly lovely and her sisters were extremely jealous of her—particularly as she was called 'Beauty' by their father. Wanting popularity more than anything, the sisters wore expensive clothes and often boasted of the family's riches. They received many offers of marriage but accepted none, claiming they could not marry unless proposed to by a prince or a nobleman.

Beauty, meanwhile, studied hard and practised the piano. Young men came to court her, but she gently explained that she was not yet ready for marriage and would spend more years helping her father.

Following some unsuccessful business ventures by the trader, he lost the whole of his fortune. Overnight he became poor, with nothing left but a little cottage far from the city. Sadly, he told his children that they needed to move there and support themselves by the work of their own hands. The man's older daughters protested strongly. Both declared they would marry quickly, even if the man was neither prince nor nobleman. They had many admirers, they said—but they were mistaken. Few men even looked at the pair now that they were poor.

People spoke of Beauty with sympathy. 'It's so sad,' they said. 'She's such a good girl—so thoughtful, polite, and kind.' Several men still wished to marry her, but Beauty couldn't think of leaving her father at such a time. Although she was sad, she said to herself, 'Tears will not give me back our riches, and one can be happy being poor.'

From the time they arrived at their country cottage,

Beauty's sisters were bored and showed only laziness. They refused to work, while Beauty rose early in the morning to wash, clean and prepare meals. The work of a servant was exhausting for her, but the exercise gave Beauty fresh health and colour. When her work was over, she amused herself by reading and singing.

'Look at Beauty,' one sister said. 'She's so stupid that she is quite content with our wretched condition.'

After one year, a letter came with wonderful news. A ship carrying goods belonging to the trader had arrived at the port. The goods had long been missing, but now he only needed to go to the city to claim them. The trader hoped he might soon be able to re-establish his business, and his daughters screamed with delight when they heard of the plan. As he was leaving, the older girls begged him to bring back new dresses and shoes. Beauty asked for nothing, for she understood that starting over would not be easy for him.

'Is there nothing you wish me to buy?' the trader enquired.

'Just a rose,' she replied. 'We have no roses growing here.'

The trader arrived at his destination to find that ownership of the goods had been contested. A court case followed and, by the end of it, he was as poor as he'd been when he had left for the city. Miserable, he set off for home. Only the thought of seeing his children again kept him going.

It was winter and, passing through a forest at night, the trader became lost. He feared he might die of cold or hunger, but when everything seemed worse than a nightmare he caught sight of a brightly lit castle. Hoping for warmth, directions and a little food—and surprised at the absence of any guards—he knocked on the door and ventured inside.

'Is anyone here?' he called. Although a fire was blazing in the hearth and there was food on the table, he heard no reply. The master of this house will not mind if I warm myself and eat a little, thought the trader. I'll explain everything, and he will pardon me.

The trader ate by the fire and began to feel sleepy. He left the dining hall, again calling out to anyone who might hear. Finally he came to a room with a comfortable bed, and he made up his mind to lie down and continue his journey in the morning.

He awoke to find fresh clothes in place of his own. Thinking the master of the castle had learnt of his presence during the

night, he looked forward to meeting him but found the dining hall empty. Even so, a hearty breakfast was set on the table and he helped himself before setting off.

Outside, there was a magnificent rose garden. Remembering Beauty's request, the trader snapped off a stem. As soon as he did so, he heard a monstrous roar and saw a Beast coming toward him. It had such a horrible appearance that he nearly fainted.

'Ungrateful man!' thundered the Beast. 'I allowed you the warmth of my fire, the food on my table, a bed for the night and the clothes you now wear. In return, you shamelessly steal one of my roses, which I care for more than anything. You must die!'

The trader fell to his knees and pleaded with the Beast. 'Forgive me, my lord. I didn't mean to offend you—I was merely picking a rose for my daughter.'

'Do not call me 'my lord',' responded the monster. 'I'm only a Beast. But you say you have daughters. Save your life by sending me one of them—if you do not, you will be killed.'

The trader had no intention of sacrificing any of his daughters to this hideous monster, but pretended to go along

with the Beast's plan. To his surprise, the Beast now spoke more kindly.

'Go now,' the Beast said. 'And remember our agreement.'

Picking up the rose he had plucked for Beauty, the trader found his way home. His children gathered around, and he wept in the knowledge that he would soon be leaving them forever. 'Take this,' he said, offering Beauty the rose. 'Your father has paid dearly for it.'

He then told his family of his terrible adventure, and the brothers insisted they would go to the castle and kill the monster.

'Impossible,' their father said. 'The Beast is so powerful that he would take your lives in a second.'

Beauty's sisters pointed their blame at her. 'Why couldn't you have asked for clothes or shoes, instead of placing our father in such danger? This is your fault.'

Beauty remained calm. 'The monster is willing to accept one of us, in exchange. I will give myself to him. The rose

picked was for me, so he can take out his anger on me. Our father picked that rose for love.'

The trader's heart was touched by Beauty's bravery. 'Beauty,' he said, 'I cannot allow you to give your life for mine.'

'But you will not return to that castle without me,' said Beauty. 'And you can't prevent me from following you. I am not afraid, and would rather be devoured by the monster than die of the sadness your death would cause me.'

The trader returned to the Beast's castle with Beauty refusing to leave his side. They found the dining table magnificently set for two. They had almost finished eating when they heard a fearful noise. The merchant shuddered, knowing it was the Beast. Beauty tried not to show fear, but the Beast looked even more horrible than she had imagined. He asked if she had come of her own free will, and seemed most surprised that she had.

'I'm obliged to you,' said the Beast. 'Your father may leave at dawn and never come back.'

Neither Beauty nor the trader felt like sleeping. The trader insisted Beauty must leave in the morning and leave him to die. She refused, and nothing her father said could persuade

her. When finally she slept, she dreamed of a good fairy who promised that her generous heart would be rewarded.

In the morning, she told her father of her dream, but it comforted him little when the Beast forced him to say goodbye. After he had gone, Beauty could not contain her tears any longer. She cried until she could cry no more. Then, believing the Beast would soon take her life, she resolved not to be glum during the short time she had left. She explored the castle, awestruck by its grandeur. To her surprise, she came to a door on which was written: *Beauty's Room*. Inside, there were fine furnishings, a bookcase and a piano.

'How nice,' Beauty said to herself. 'But all I wish is to see my father again.'

Magically, a large mirror offered her a picture of her home and her father returning to it. Her sisters ran to meet him and she saw their delight in having lost their sister in place of him. Just as mysteriously, the mirror looked ordinary again. Even so, the experience left Beauty with a feeling that the Beast may not be as nasty as he seemed.

That evening she was sitting down to her meal when she heard the Beast's voice. 'Beauty,' he said to her, 'will you allow me to watch while you are eating your dinner?'

'You are my master,' replied Beauty, trembling.

'Not so,' said the Beast. 'If I annoy you, tell me to leave and I will go at once.' He paused before asking in a voice that seemed almost timid: 'Tell me truthfully, do you think I'm very ugly?'

'I do,' said Beauty. 'But I also think you may be kind, and that I have nothing to fear.'

'Besides being ugly, I am also stupid.'

'No one is stupid,' Beauty remarked. 'Especially those who understand there is much to learn.'

'Eat,' said the monster. 'Try to find pleasure in your own house. I want you to be happy.'

'You are indeed kind,' Beauty told him.

'I may have a kind heart, but for all that I am a monster.'

'Many men are bigger monsters than you,' said Beauty. 'And I care more for the kind-hearted than those whose pleasant faces hide rotten hearts.' Though she had lost almost all her fear of the monster, she nearly died of fright when he spoke again.

'Beauty, will you be my wife?'

She sat for a while without answering, not wanting to stir his anger by refusing him. Finally she said, 'No, Beast.' The poor monster sighed, and the hideous sound he made echoed throughout the castle. When he turned and left the room, Beauty felt pity for him. 'Alas!' she said, 'it is a shame he is so ugly, for he is good.'

The Beast paid Beauty a visit every evening as she ate her dinner. Beauty discovered many good qualities in the monster and, far from fearing his visit, looked forward to it. But before leaving, the Beast would ask again if she would be his wife, sighing deeply when she refused.

One night, Beauty told him: 'I am too truthful to make you believe that marriage is possible, but I shall always be your friend. I hope you will be satisfied with that.'

'If I must,' responded the Beast. 'I know I am horrible to look at, but I love you deeply. At least promise me that you'll never leave.'

'I would,' Beauty said to him, 'but I will die of sorrow if I cannot see my father again.'

'Then I will send you home to your father and you may stay

there,' said the monster. 'Your poor Beast will die of loneliness in your absence.'

'No!' said Beauty, crying. 'I care for you and promise to return. Your magic mirror has allowed me to see that my sisters are finally married, and that my brothers have entered the army. My father is alone—let me be with him for just one week.'

'Very well,' said the Beast with his usual sigh. 'One week. You will wake tomorrow morning in his house. To return, place your ring on the table before going to bed and you'll be transported back here.'

Beauty awoke next morning at home. Her father cried with joy to find his youngest daughter returned to him alive, and was happy to know that the Beast had treated her with kindness and respect. News of Beauty's arrival was sent to her sisters, who were most unhappy. The first had married a handsome man so in love with himself that he took little notice of her. The second had married a man with a sharp tongue who put everybody in a bad temper, beginning with his wife. They were more jealous than ever when they saw Beauty dressed like a princess, happy and as beautiful as ever.

When alone, they complained bitterly.

'Why should she be happier than we are? It is so unfair!'

'I have an idea,' said the other sister. 'Let's keep her here longer than a week. Her stupid old Beast will be so angry that he may kill her, or at least throw her out forever.'

The sisters set about making Beauty feel greatly loved and, when the week drew to a close, showed such signs of grief that she promised to stay a few extra days. Beauty felt guilty for causing her poor Beast pain and, on the tenth night of her absence, dreamed that he was on his deathbed. She woke with a start.

I am wicked, she thought. *The Beast has been considerate and kind to me! It's not his fault that he is ugly. He has character, honesty and generosity, and these are worth more than anything else. Why did I refuse to marry him? I would be happier with him than my sisters are with their husbands. If I make him unhappy, I shall never forgive myself.*

Beauty placed her ring on the table and, next morning, awoke in the Beast's castle. The hours until dinner dragged, but, when the time came, the Beast did not appear. Beauty feared the worst and ran through the castle, calling out

frantically. Eventually she found him, collapsed beside his beloved rose garden. Forgetting her horror at his appearance, she threw herself upon him. His heart was still beating, so she fetched water and threw it over his head.

The Beast opened his eyes. 'I have starved myself but will die happy,' he said weakly. 'I had lost hope of seeing you again.'

'You must not die,' exclaimed Beauty. 'You shall be my husband. I thought the feeling I had for you was only friendship, but it is true love.'

As soon as she finished speaking, fireworks exploded in the sky. Beauty did not gaze long at them and turned her eyes back to her Beast, but he was beast no longer. Instead, he was a handsome Prince. He rose and thanked her. Her love had released him from an evil spell.

'A witch condemned me to living in the form of a monster until someone agreed to marry me,' he explained. 'And I was also forbidden from showing intelligence. You let the simple goodness of my heart touch yours.'

Beauty was overwhelmed. She gave the Prince her hand and they went into the castle. Now, her whole family was assembled in the dining hall. She also saw the good fairy who had promised that her generosity would be rewarded.

'Beauty,' said the fairy, 'you preferred kindness to beauty or intelligence. You deserve to find all those qualities in one person. You will marry your Prince and become a great Queen.'

The fairy turned to Beauty's sisters. 'You are petty and selfish, and shall become statues. If you truly feel shame over your faults, your flesh will be restored—but it is not easy to repair mean spirit and jealous hearts.' With two quick taps of her wand, the sisters were turned to stone.

Beauty married her loving Prince, who provided all that her father and brothers might want. They lived happily ever after.

Also read Volume 1 of All-time Favourite Fairy Tales 5-in-1 by Ken Spillman

Sleeping Beauty
Jack and the Beanstalk
The Ugly Duckling
Cinderella
The Three Little Pigs

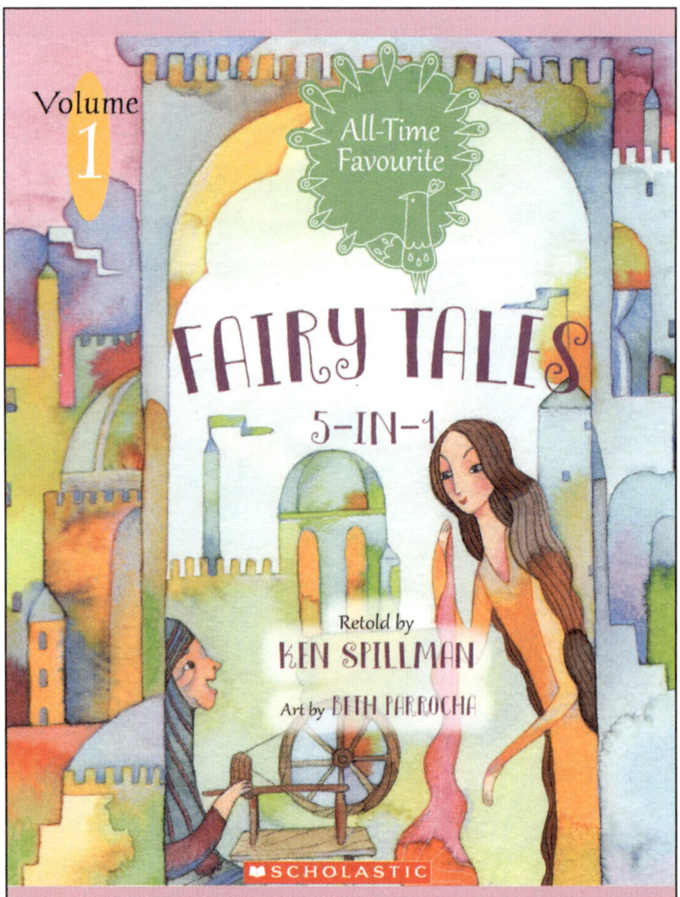